Dear mouse friends,
Welcome to the world of

Geronimo Stilton

THE RODENT'S GAZETTE
EDITORIAL STAFF

Geronimo Stilton
A learned and brainy
mouse; editor of
The Rodent's Gazette

Thea Stilton
Geronimo's sister and
special correspondent at
The Rodent's Gazette

Trap Stilton
An awful joker;
Geronimo's cousin and
owner of the store
Cheap Junk for Less

Benjamin Stilton
A sweet and loving
nine-year-old mouse;
Geronimo's favorite
nephew

Geronimo Stilton

GERONIMO'S VALENTINE

Scholastic Inc.

New York   Toronto   London   Auckland   Sydney

Mexico City   New Delhi   Hong Kong   Buenos Aires

No part of this publication may be reproduced, stored in a retrieval system, or transmitted in any form or by any means, electronic, mechanical, photocopying, recording, or otherwise, without written permission from the copyright holder. For information regarding permission, please contact: Atlantyca S.p.A., Via Leopardi 8, 20123 Milan, Italy; e-mail foreignrights@atlantyca.it, www.atlantyca.com.

ISBN 978-0-545-02136-4

Copyright © 2009 by Edizioni Piemme S.p.A., Via Tiziano 32, 20145 Milan, Italy.

International Rights © Atlantyca S.p.A.

English translation © 2009 by Atlantyca S.p.A.

GERONIMO STILTON names, characters, and related indicia are copyright, trademark, and exclusive license of Atlantyca S.p.A. All rights reserved. The moral right of the author has been asserted.

Based on an original idea by Elisabetta Dami.

www.geronimostilton.com

Published by Scholastic Inc., 557 Broadway, New York, NY 10012. SCHOLASTIC and associated logos are trademarks and/or registered trademarks of Scholastic Inc.

Stilton is the name of a famous English cheese. It is a registered trademark of the Stilton Cheese Makers' Association. For more information, go to www.stiltoncheese.com

Text by Geronimo Stilton
Original title *Lo strano caso del tiramisù*
Cover by Giuseppe Ferrario
Illustrations by Giuseppe Ferrario
Graphics by Merenguita Gingermouse and Yuko Egusa

Special thanks to Kathryn Cristaldi
Translated by Lidia Morson Tramontozzi
Interior design by Kay Petronio

18 17 16   13 14 15 16/0

Printed in the U.S.A.   40
First printing, January 2009

A VERY
SPECIAL DATE

I scampered home from work extra early to get ready. I had so many things to do — take a shower, comb my whiskers, and get dressed. After all, it was a very special day. It was Valentine's Day, and I had a very important date. I was so excited, I could barely squeak!

Can you guess the name of my valentine?

Well, her name is . . .

Oops! I almost forgot to introduce myself. My name is Stilton, *Geronimo Stilton*. I am the publisher of the most famouse newspaper on Mouse Island, *The Rodent's Gazette*.

Anyway, where was I? Oh, yes, I was about to tell you about my valentine. Her name is

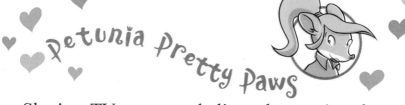

She is a TV reporter dedicated to saving the environment. What a FASCINATING rodent! I have had a crush on her for the longest time.

The phone rang just as I was getting into the shower. It was my friend Hercule Poirat, Mouse Island's most famous detective.

"Stilton, I need your help solving a **CHEESECAKE MYSTERY**," he began.

I cut him off gently.

"Sorry, Hercule," I squeaked. "I'm busy. I'll call you back."

I hung up the phone and hopped into the shower. Ah, don't you just love a nice, steamy shower? I washed my fur ten times. By the time I was done, my paws were wrinkled and there was no more hot water. Oh, well. At least I was squeaky clean. I combed my whiskers, popped a breath mint in my mouth, and sprayed myself with

my favorite cologne, **Cheddarini**: For the *Sophisticated* Rodent. Then I put on my *tuxedo*. I had rented it just for the occasion.

I looked at my watch. Only **TWO HOURS** until our date. I couldn't wait!

WHO DID THAT???

Besides the tuxedo, I had also rented a *posh* new cheese-colored **CONVERTIBLE**. I was hoping Petunia would be impressed. Did I mention I have a terrible crush on her? She's so **beautiful**, so **charming**, so **delightful**. Too bad I can't tell my left paw  from my right when I'm around her. Still, I told myself that tonight would be different.

"Tonight I will ask Petunia to be my ♥**valentine**!" I squeaked, giving myself a quick pep talk.

I glanced at my watch. Only **O N E** **H O U R** until our date. I tried a few deep breathing exercises to relax myself. Then I checked the time again. Better early than late, I decided.

As I was walking out of my house, a pail of **rotten** fish rained down on my head. So much for my expensive cologne! The pail had fallen from the roof, so I looked up.

"Who did that?" I yelled. But no one answered.

I ran back inside, took a **freezing** cold shower, and ran out again. Two seconds later, I was flying down the stairs outside my building. Someone had left a banana peel on the steps. I slipped and flipped through the air. When I landed, I split my **pants**.

How humiliating. How embarrassing. How strange. I hadn't seen that banana peel when I came out of my house the first time.

"**Who did that?**" I shrieked. But no one answered.

I charged back inside and changed into my everyday green suit. My date was turning into a disaster before it even began! *Calm down, Geronimo,* I told myself as I climbed into the cheese-colored convertible. A second later, a dump truck drove by and spilled an entire load of yucky mud on me!

"Rat-munching rattlesnakes!" I cried. "**Who did that?**"

From inside the dump truck, a familiar face emerged. It was my friend Hercule Poirat!

"I got you, Stilton!" he chuckled. "I'm so good at pulling pranks."

I was so mad steam poured from my ears. I glared at Hercule.

He didn't seem to notice. "I'm here to get your **help** with this CHEESECAKE

MYSTERY I need to solve." he said.

I forced myself not to pull out all of my fur. "Listen, Hercule," I said. "I already told you, it's *Valentine's Day*, and I have a very important date."

I stared miserably at my posh **sports car** filled with mud and my stained green suit. "You've **ruined** my car and my clothes." I wailed.

"Aw, come on, Geronimo," Hercule said. "It's not that bad. If you want, I'll lend you my **dump truck**."

I burst into tears. What's worse than driving to a date in a car filled with mud? Driving to a date in a dump truck!

Finally, I pulled myself together. What else could I do? Petunia was waiting.

On top of everything else, I was LATE for my date!

DO YOU SMELL RAW FISH?

I ran back home and took another **frozen** shower. I threw on an old **JOGGING** outfit. It was the only clean thing I had left. (I knew I should have done my **laundry** the night before!) Then I raced back outside. I was about to call a taxi when I remembered something. Something awful. The cabs and buses were all on **STRIKE**! My fur stood on end. Holey cheese! I felt like I was about to explode. At that moment, I spotted my nephew Benjamin's **bicycle**. It would have to do.

I **JUMPED** on and began pedaling furiously. I was supposed to meet Petunia at Le Squeakery. It was my **FAVORITE** restaurant, in the heart of New Mouse City. By the time I got there, I was sweating like a contestant on *America's Next Top Stuntmouse*. I glanced at my watch.

Cheese nibblets!

I was two hours late.

The manager greeted me at the door with a **HORRIFIED** look on his snout.

"Mr. Stilton, you're not wearing a tie," he squeaked. "You know we have a dress code."

I *strode* past him. I didn't care about the manager. I didn't care about the dress code. I had to see Petunia. I had to apologize for being so late.

I started *running* through the restaurant. The waiters tried to stop me, but I **dodged** past them. I was like a mouse in a pinball machine, bouncing from table to table. As I ran, I could hear the shocked comments from the other diners.

"Isn't that *Stilton*, the famous publisher? Why is he dressed like that?"

"He looks like he escaped from the Mad Mouse Center."

"DO YOU SMELL RAW FISH?"

How embarrassing!

When Petunia saw me, she gasped.

"Geronimo! What happened?" she asked. "You're two hours **LATE** and you stink like fish!"

My fur turned **Beet RED**.

"I'm so sorry, Nepunia. I mean, Tenupa, I mean, Petunia. The fish, I mean the car, I mean the banana peel . . ." I muttered. Oh, why did I always have to sound like a **FOOL** in front of Petunia?

She got up from the table, annoyed.

"I'm sorry, too, Geronimo," she huffed. "I thought I was *important* to you, but now I see I was wrong."

I was about to run after her when guess who showed up? That's right — Hercule Poirat!

"Is now a good time to talk about the **CHEESECAKE MYSTERY**, Geronimo?" he asked. "I see your date just ditched you."

I WANTED TO SCREAM.

I wanted to cry. I wanted to pull out my whiskers.

Instead I headed for the door. I was so depressed I didn't notice Hercule's tail in front of me. I tripped and landed snout-first in an enormous pan of macaroni and cheese.

The waiters picked me up and threw me out.

Happy Valentine's Day to me!

A CALL IN
THE NIGHT

By the time I got home, it was **TEN O'CLOCK**.

I **was beat.** I fell into bed with all of my clothes on. I was snoring away when the phone *rang*.

"Gilton, *Steronimo Gilton*," I stammered, still half asleep.

At the other end, I heard Hercule's voice.

"Is now a good time, Geronimo?" he squeaked. "I really could use your help with the **CHEESECAKE MYSTERY**."

I stared at my Cheeseball the Clown alarm clock with bleary eyes.

It was four in the morning. All I wanted to do was climb back under my Great-aunt Ratsy's down comforter and go back to

sleep. But something told me that wasn't going to happen. Hercule would keep bugging me until I gave in.

"Okay, Hercule," I agreed. "You win. I'll meet you at your house in twenty minutes."

"Make it ten," my *friend* insisted. "After all, the early mouse gets the cheese."

I hung up the phone with a groan.

Then I rolled out of bed, brushed my teeth, and threw on my STINKY clothes. I am usually such a squeaky-clean mouse, but what else could I do? I had no time to do laundry. I had no time to shower. I barely had time to **comb** my own FUR. Oh, when would this smelly nightmare end?

THE CELEBRATION OF CHOCOLATE CHEESECAKE

Hercule was waiting for me, pacing **up** and **down**, in front of his house. He was staring at his watch. "You're one minute late, Stilton," he scolded when he saw me. "It's really rude to keep your friends waiting, you know."

I chewed my whiskers to keep from squeaking. It was so early, the **sun** was still sleeping! I followed Hercule into his house and **sank** into a pawchair. Did I mention I'm not much of a morning mouse?

My friend didn't seem to notice. "Okay, Stilton, here's the scoop," he squeaked. "Yesterday, I got a call from Kristina

Colorsnout. You know Kristina, right?"

I nodded my head. Of course I knew Kristina. She was the assistant director of the NEW MOUSE CITY MOUSEUM OF ART. Ah, how I love that museum. It is filled with spectacular paintings by the most famous artists in New Mouse City. I am always taking trips to the museum with my nephew Benjamin.

"Anyway, Kristina called to tell me about a terrible BURGLARY," Hercule continued. "It seems someone has stolen an original Passionpaw. And not just any Passionpaw — they took The Celebration of Chocolate Cheesecake!"

The Celebration
of Chocolate
Cheesecake

NOTE: PAINTING NOT YET RESTORED.

I gasped. Pierre Passionpaw was one of Mouse Island's most distinguished painters from long ago. *The Celebration of Chocolate Cheesecake* was featured in **every** art history book. It showed the founder of New Mouse City, **Grant Gentlemouse,** and his bride, **Glitterfur,** on their wedding day. In the painting, Gentlemouse is offering his new wife a sample of a brand-new **dessert: CHOCOLATE CHEESECAKE.**

Just thinking about cheesecake made my tummy rumble.

I was starving.

"Uh, do you think we have time to swing by the **Squeak and Chew**?" I asked Hercule. "I just realized I never ate dinner last night."

Hercule looked annoyed. "**How can you think about food at a time like this?!**" he shrieked. "We have to find that painting

fast. The museum is holding an important *ceremony* tomorrow afternoon at four thirty. If we don't find it by then, Ms. Colorsnout will be in big **TROUBLE**!"

Then he blushed. "Plus, Ms. Colorsnout is a good friend of my granny Ironwhiskers and I promised Granny I'd **SOLVE** the mystery," he said, looking embarrassed. "Granny can get pretty upset if she doesn't get her way. Trust me, she can drive a mouse right up a clock!"

Granny Ironwhiskers, Hercule's grandmother

Kristina Colorsnout, the museum's assistant director

OFF IN THE BANANAMOBILE!

Two minutes later, with my tummy still grumbling, we took off in Hercule's **Bananamobile**. Have you ever seen a Bananamobile? It is a very **unique** car.

It's **YELLOW** and it's shaped just like a real **banana**. It doesn't **pollute** the air because the motor runs on banana peels. Isn't that neat? My friend Hercule is totally into the **environment**.

Too bad he's not into obeying the rules of the road. I hung on for dear life as we **SPED** through an intersection. Headlines flashed inside my head: STILTON SQUASHED ON WILD BANANA RIDE! PUBLISHER KILLED IN FRUITY CAR CRASH!

By the time we got to the museum, I felt sick.

"You look a little green, Stilton," Hercule observed. "Drink this. It will give you **ENERGY**."

He opened a thermos and poured a yucky-smelling liquid into a cup.

I took a sip.

"**Cheese nibblets!**" I squeaked. The drink was not only disgusting — it was **BURNING HOT!**

I thought I would never taste

Cheese nibblets!

cheddar again.
My tastebuds were
FRIED. I began
to sob loudly.

Keep it down!

Hercule slapped his
paw over my mouth.

"Keep it down, Geronimo. We're on a
top-secret case!" he scolded.

I hung my head. I was a **miserable** mess.
I was tired. I was hungry. And my tongue
was about to fall out of my mouth.

Could things get any worse?

Youch!

I followed Hercule out of the car.
Then it happened. Things got
worse.

As I was climbing
out of the car, Hercule
SHUT the door on my
tail.

"**YOoooucch!**" I wailed at the top of my lungs.

Hercule slapped his paw over my mouth.

"Quiet, Geronimo! Remember: top secret!" he hissed.

He whipped out a **FLASHLIGHT** and took off down a dark alley. I followed closely behind him. I didn't want to be left behind. It was so dark. My fur was standing on end. Did I mention I'm a bit of a scaredy mouse?

Suddenly, my friend stopped.

"Here it is. The back door to the museum," he whispered.

He waved the flashlight in the air, **SMACKING** me in the snout.

"**Owwwwwwwawwww!**" I screeched.

Hercule slapped his paw over my mouth.

"What is wrong with you, Geronimo?" he growled. "Can't you stay quiet for two minutes?"

I twisted my tail in a knot to keep from shrieking. My tongue was throbbing, my tail ached, and now my snout was turning all shades of purple. Who knew hanging out with Mouse Island's most famous detective could be so dangerous!

PASSWORD:
CHOCOLATE CHEESY
CHEWS

I was still rubbing my sore snout when Hercule knocked on the door **THREE** times.

A voice floated out from behind the door. "Password?"

Hercule bent close to the door.

"Chocolate Cheesy Chews," he whispered.

My mouth began to water. Have you ever had a chocolate cheesy chew? It is the most whisker-licking, *delicious* kind of candy. I was starting to drool when the door popped open. How embarrassing!

The face of an old and worried rodent appeared. It was **Kristina** Colorsnout.

She wore a **green** dress with a gold brooch. Her fur was pinned back into a bun. She looked so frail and sad, I felt sorry for her.

I took her paw.

"I'm not sure if you remember me or not, Ms. Colorsnout," I said. "My name is Stilton. *Geronimo Stilton. What can I do for you?*"

Kristina Colorsnout brightened. "Of course I remember you, Geronimo," she

Ms. Colorsnout...

What a gentlemouse!

squeaked. "And how is your sweet nephew Benjamin?"

I began to answer, but Hercule cut me off.

"I hate to break up this party, but time is ticking and we have important work to do," he interrupted. "Now Ms. Colorsnout, please tell us exactly when you realized the painting was **MISSING**."

Kristina's face fell, and her paws began to tremble. She led us down a long corridor to a **huge** gallery. Then she began to tell her story. "It all started when I sent the painting out to be restored," she began.

BUT THEN . . .
BUT THEN . . .
BUT THEN . . .

Kristina explained that the **painting** was in terrible shape. The **colors** had faded, and it was covered with dust.

"Luckily, I just happen to know the best expert in **restoration** in all of Mouse Island. Her name is **Perky Le Mouse**. The painting was taken to the museum's lab.

Perky Le Mouse

Perky worked on it for six months, DAY and **NIGHT**. Yesterday, she called me. She couldn't wait to show me the results. It was to be **unveiled** at tomorrow's ceremony," Kristina squeaked, **tears** rolling down her fur. "But then . . . but then . . . but then . . ."

She stopped to blow her nose. Then she **cried** some more.

"But what?" Hercule asked. He stared at his watch. He tapped his paw. He chewed his *whiskers*. I could tell he was getting really impatient. Maybe I could teach him a few breathing exercises to help him relax. He looked like he was about to tear out all of his fur and run around the room squeaking like a MADMOUSE.

Finally, Kristina went on. "Perky told me she had discovered something very strange about the painting. Something extremely important. She wanted to tell me in person. But when I got to the lab, she was GONE. The window was wide open, and the painting had VANISHED! Tomorrow night, there will be a celebration to show off the restored painting. Mayor Bigmouse will be there, along

with all of my coworkers. *Oh, what am I going to do?"*

Kristina began to <u>sob</u> uncontrollably. I felt awful. Here I was feeling sorry for myself because I had to get up early and my tummy was rumbling. What a CHEESEHEAD I'd been. I promised myself I'd help Hercule find that missing painting even if I had to skip my afternoon snack. Well, maybe I'd have one little nibble. Or maybe two. Three tops. What can I

say? I think much better on a full stomach.

I patted Kristina on the shoulder. "Don't worry, Ms. Colorsnout," I said. "We'll find out what happened."

Hercule took out his notebook. "Do you suspect anybody?" he asked. Kristina shook her head. Then she showed us a PHOTO of Perky Le Mouse.

She looked so *sweet*. We just had to find her.

But how do you find a stolen painting and a missing mouse?

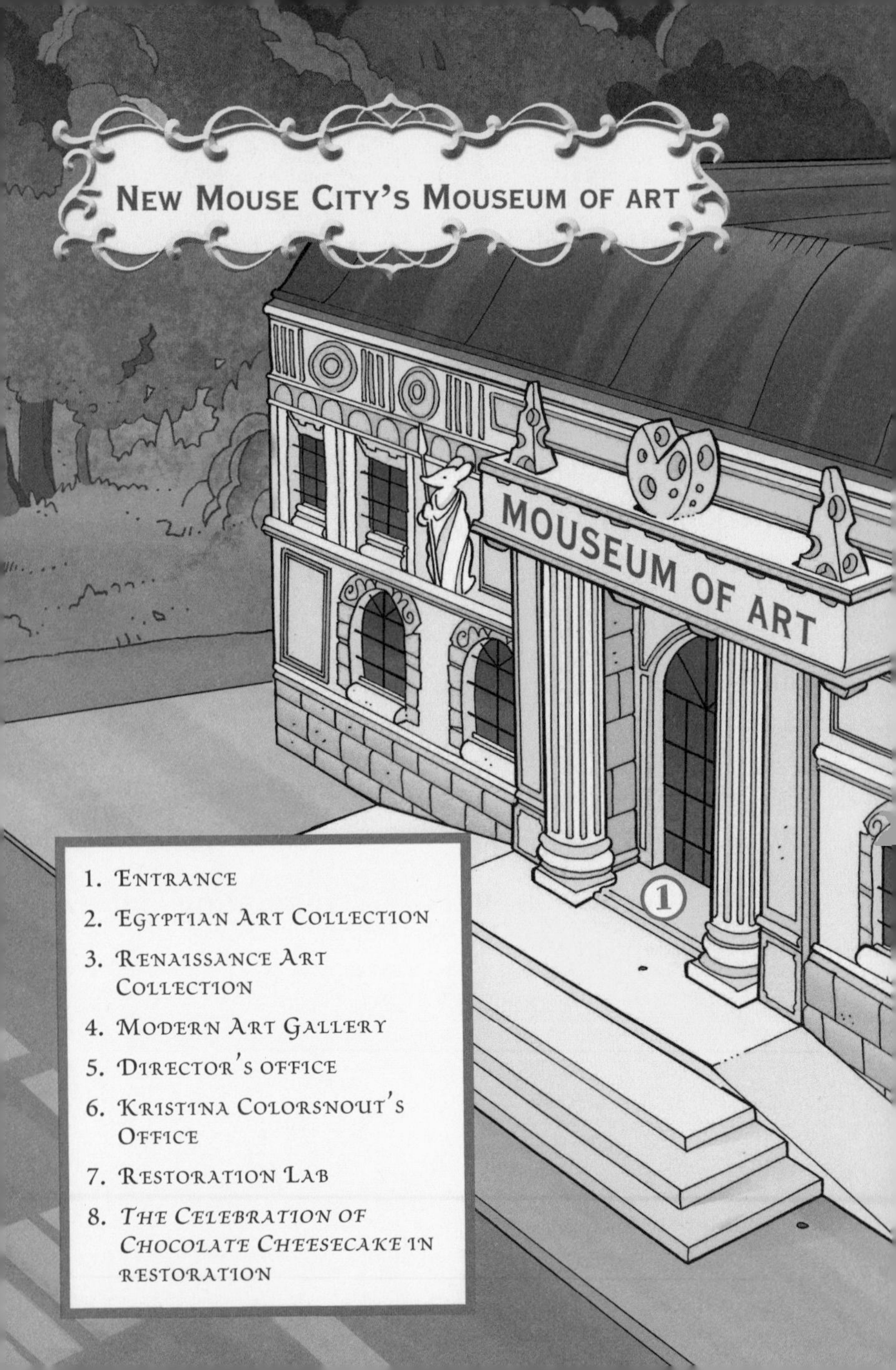

New Mouse City's Mouseum of Art
MOUSEUM OF ART
1
1. Entrance
2. Egyptian Art Collection
3. Renaissance Art Collection
4. Modern Art Gallery
5. Director's office
6. Kristina Colorsnout's Office
7. Restoration Lab
8. The Celebration of Chocolate Cheesecake in restoration

GOTCHA!

As soon as we left the gallery, Hercule sprang into action. At least someone knew what to do.

"Before we hit the lab, let's take a **QUICK LOOK** around the museum," he instructed.

We split up. Hercule went **RIGHT**. I went **LEFT**.

I scampered down the dark hallway. My heart started to pound. It was so **SPOOKY**. Did I mention I'm afraid of the dark, loud noises, and **pink bubble gum**? I once had a wad of bubble gum stuck in my fur. It took Clip Rat, my barber, three hours to cut it all out. What a nightmare. Oh, but that's another story.

Anyway, where was I? Ah, yes, in the museum. I passed by tons of **PRICELESS**

artifacts. Each one was more amazing than the next.

Here was the hat that had been worn by the founder of New Mouse City. And there was the shovel that was used to lay the first stone for City Hall. Then I turned a corner and saw it. No, I'm not talking about another ancient treasure. I'm talking about a **SHADOW**. It slid toward me . . . closer and closer. I could hardly believe it. WAS IT THE THIEF?

Before I could SCREAM, a spiky **MALLET** that

looked like it was from medieval times bonked me over the head.

"**Gotcha!**" a familiar voice announced.

I let out a loud yelp. "Hercule!" I cried, shining the flashlight in his snout. "WHat are you Doing Here? I thought you went right."

What are you doing here?

Hercule looked surprised. "I did go **RIGHT**. But then I changed my mind and decided to go **LEFT**."

"Then why didn't you **WARN** me?" I shrieked.

"You know that's the way I am: very **UNPreDiCtaBLe**," Hercule replied. "Plus, I wanted to surprise the thief. I thought you were him."

I took off my glasses so I could cry freely. My head was **THROBBING**, and I had a **lump** the size of a watermelon on my head.

At the rate things were going, I'd be a dead mouse before lunchtime!

My head was throbbing!

MOUSENAPPED!

Finally, we reached the restoration lab of the museum. In the center, there was an EMPTY easel.

"Hmmm," Hercule said thoughtfully. "Ms. Colorsnout said that the painting was on this easel while it was being worked on."

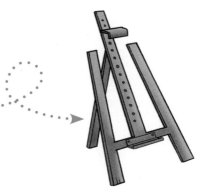

Next to it was a dirty, color-stained rag soaked in a strange liquid that smelled awful.

ᴄᴇ WHAT DOES ᴐᴎ
RESTORATION MEAN?

Restoration means bringing works of art back to their original beauty. It also means safe-guarding them through time.

All around us there are monuments, buildings, paintings, and manuscripts that describe our past. Preserving these artifacts over time keeps the story of our civilization alive.

There are universities and restoration schools that teach this skill. This type of work requires **patience and dedication**.

In 1984, restoration began on the famous Statue of Liberty to repair thousands of small holes and dents in the statue's copper surface. The holes were caused by 100 years of exposure to salty sea air. The two-year restoration project also included work to strengthen the statue's iron framework, which had been distorted over the previous century.

The object of restoring a painting is to recreate the form and colors that have been damaged by time, weather, or other elements. X-rays are often used to analyze the techniques used by the artist. X-rays are also used to determine whether a painting is authentic and to tell if there's another work of art painted under it. X-rays can also reveal the various phases the artist went through while he or she worked on the piece of artwork.

The ODOR was so **STRONG** I had to hold my nose to keep from fainting. But not Hercule. He marched right up to the dirty rag and examined it.

He explained that the rag was soaked in turpentine, a substance that is used to **DISSOLVE** paint. "It's as if someone took off some of the paint . . . but why?" he wondered aloud.

He searched the laboratory and found a purse. It belonged to Perky Le Mouse. Inside, Hercule discovered her wallet, her cell phone, and her car keys.

"Why would she leave this behind?" I asked.

Hercule looked at me gravely. "There's only one explanation," he squeaked. "Perky Le Mouse must have been mousenapped!

A chill ran down my fur. Mousenapped! Playing detective was no joke. This was serious business.

I was still thinking about Perky when Hercule let out an **excited** shout.

He was leaning out the open window, pointing to a trail of **pawprints** in the dirt.

"This is it!" he squeaked. "This is where the thief must have fled. And look what I found on the windowsill."

Hercule held up a tiny piece of paper. It said:

SUGARHOG
CHEESECAKE
FACTORY
SQUEAKS SUGARHOG
Owner
25 Foodie Avenue
New Mouse City, Mouse Island 13131

It was **Squeaks Sugarhog's** business card! Squeaks was the owner of the biggest and most successful cheesecake factory on Mouse Island. He was a very private, very **Mysterious** mouse. In fact, no one on Mouse Island had ever even seen him. The only thing we knew about Squeaks was that he was EXTREMELY RICH.

Hercule stared intently at the business card. Then he clapped his paws.

"Fabumouse!" he cried. "I just realized something. Squeaks's factory is right across the street from the museum. I think it's time to pay the mysterious Squeaks Sugarhog a little visit. I **smell** something fishy."

THE MYSTERIOUS CHEESECAKE FACTORY

We left the museum and scampered across the street to the factory. It was **6** **A.M.**

Luckily for us, no one was around. Hercule pointed to an open **WINDOW**. A minute later, we were inside the factory. The aroma of sugary *desserts* filled our nostrils. The smell was so overpowering, it gave me an instant sugar headache. It was so unfair. I hadn't even eaten one lick of a jelly **doughnut** yet today. I tried to figure out where we were, but it was too **DARK**. I couldn't even see my paw in front of my face! To make things worse, Hercule refused to let me use my flashlight.

"I'm like a **CAT**. I can see perfectly well

in the dark," he boasted. Then he poked me in the eye.

"OUUUUUUUCH!" I yelped.

Hercule slapped his paw over my mouth to keep me quiet.

"If I let you turn on your flashlight, do you think you can keep it down?" he hissed.

"Mmmfl Mmmfl," I spluttered into his paw.

I flicked on my light. **WOW!**

The factory was **ENORMOUSE**.

I could see mountains of **EGGS**,

huge metal **VATS** filled with

cream cheese, massive bins

packed with *sugar*,

tubs of **MELTED CHOCOLATE**,

and **GIGANTIC** refrigerators all around the room. High above the equipment, a metal walkway ran around the entire room.

Hercule waved me over to a **ladder**. "We'll see much better from up there," he insisted.

I gulped. Did I mention I'm afraid of heights?

1. SERVICE ENTRANCE
2. SUGAR
3. REFRIGERATORS
4. CHOCOLATE
5. CREAM CHEESE
6. EGGS
7. SQUEAKS SUGARHOG'S SECRET ROOM
8. TRAPDOOR

I started creeping up the
ladder on shaky paws. Just
as I reached the top, Hercule

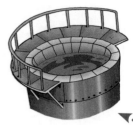

SLIPPED, accidentally kicking me. I went
flying headfirst into an enormous vat of hot,
melted chocolate chips. ....

"Youch!" I cried. Hercule reached down to
pull me out of the vat. But he pulled too

hard. I flipped over the railing
and landed in a tub of cream
cheese. "Help!" I gasped,
my mouth full of cream cheese.
"Really, Stilton, if you're that
hungry, I've got a cheese stick in
my pocket," Hercule scolded.

I was about to respond when I heard
a strange whirring sound. Holey cheese!
Hercule must have leaned against a button
and started the *blender*. I was being

sucked into the cream cheese!
I wanted to squeak! I wanted
to shout! As the blender
SPUN, graham cracker crust crumbs
pelted me in the head as they tumbled into
the vat. With my last bit of strength, I dragged
myself to safety.

"**WOW, THAT WAS SO COOL**,"

Hercule chuckled. "You
looked like you were in a
giant bubbling Jacuzzi."
He picked up something
that resembled a giant blow-dryer. "Here,
I'll dry you off," he suggested. Before I could
stop him, he hit a switch. A tornado of
cocoa powder enveloped me. "Oops,"
said Hercule, hitting the switch again. He
swiped at my fur, then stuck his paw in his
mouth. "**DELICIOUS!**" he announced.

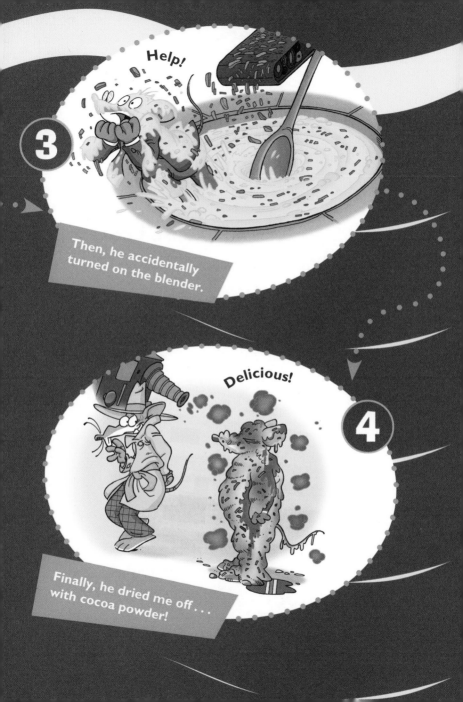

A SECRET PASSAGEWAY

Suddenly we heard a sound. **Footsteps** were coming from somewhere up above. We were both *shocked*.

"Maybe there's a floor hidden between the ceiling and the roof," Hercule suggested. "There might be a *secret* passageway."

I began to gently knock on the wall behind us.

Just then I stopped. "I found it!" I squeaked. My **EYES** widened as a section of the wall slid open to reveal a long, **DARK** staircase.

My teeth began to **chatter**. Why were there no lights in this place? Didn't anyone believe in *electricity* anymore?

SQUEAKS SUGARHOG

I started to squeak about the dark, but Hercule wasn't listening. So we SCAMPERED up the staircase. At the top of the staircase, there was a trapdoor. Hercule pushed it open.

I closed my eyes. What would we find? A slobbering monster?

I opened my eyes. No monster. But we did spot a tall, skinny rodent. He was scurrying along a **LONG, DARK, NARROW HALLWAY** toward a brightly lit room.

We followed as quietly as mice.

Two seconds later, the rodent slipped into the room. Luckily for us, he left the door open. We peeked inside.

The room was empty except for one long

dining table. It looked like it was set for a fancy banquet, with a huge centerpiece and glittering GOLD candlesticks. On the wall hung three paintings. How odd. They all were of the same **large**, rather stern-looking mouse. It had to be Squeaks Sugarhog. I was so busy looking at the paintings, I didn't notice the **large**, rather stern-looking mouse sitting at the far end of the table. He was dressed in an expensive pin-striped suit and wore a scowl on his snout. It was **Squeaks Sugarhog**!

Suddenly, he began shouting at the skinny rodent. "What took you so long, Furbrain?!" he shrieked. "I'm dying of hunger here!"

The skinny rodent, who wore a butler's uniform, raced over to Squeaks. He heaped some thick, cheesy soup into a **HUGE BOWL**.

My stomach rumbled just looking at it! Then the **butler** stepped back. Good thing! Squeaks shoveled in his food so fast, half of it missed his mouth. Some stuck to his fur. Some splattered on the floor. What a **slob**! Squeaks really needed to take a class with my friend Daintyfur. Daintyfur teaches classes on etiquette at the Cheddartown Y. She's really **amazing**. I always tell her she could teach a sewer rat to behave. I was sure she could help Squeaks.

I pulled out my wallet to search for Daintyfur's business card when Hercule smacked me. He pointed to the skinny butler. It was then that I noticed a small window cut into the wall by one of the paintings. The butler was using a telescope to look out the window. How sneaky! Squeaks must have built this room so he could **spy** on his own factory **workers**.

At that moment, the butler cleared his throat. "Er . . . um . . . excuse me Mr. Sugarhog, sir, but . . . um . . . I was wondering if you might um, consider giving me a raise now that I . . . er . . . **stole** that **painting** for you," he stammered.

Squeaks slammed his paw on the table.

"Forget about it, you fool!" he cried. "I can't afford it. I just bought myself a solid GOLD luxury town car. Now bring me that painting before I fire you!"

RECIPE
UNDER A ROCK

The butler ran away.

A minute later, he returned with a wrapped package. He gave it to Squeaks, who tore it open with greedy paws.

IT WAS THE MISSING PAINTING!

But something about the painting was *different*. It looked like someone had written their grocery list in the corner!

Squeaks slammed his paw on the table. He looked very angry. "What happened to the painting? Who is responsible for this? Get me that restorer!" he **squeaked** at the top of his lungs.

THE PERFECT CHOCOLATE CHEESECAKE

CRUST:
1 1/2 cups chocolate wafer crumbs
1/4 teaspoon ground cinnamon
6 tablespoons butter or margarine, melted

FILLING:
4 8-ounce packages cream cheese
1 cup sugar
1 tablespoon flour
5 eggs
1/2 cup sour cream
12 ounces semisweet chocolate chips, melted
2 teaspoons vanilla extract

The butler quickly disappeared and returned with a young mouse. She had a *sweet* face and she looked frightened.

I checked the photo Ms. Colorsnout had given us. It was Perky Le Mouse!

"I want an explanation!" **THUNDERED** Squeaks. "Why on earth would you write on a priceless painting?"

Perky shook her head.

"Oh, no, Mr. Sugarhog," she replied. "I didn't write on the painting. The artist did. You see, while I was restoring the painting, I noticed something strange. The **ROCK** in the corner of the picture seemed to have many layers of **PAINT** on it. I dipped a rag into turpentine and removed the top layer. What I found was amazing. The artist had written a recipe on the painting. It's a recipe for the **PERFECT CHOCOLATE CHEESECAKE**."

Squeaks went from mad to **glad** in about three point two seconds. "This is more than amazing!" he exclaimed. "It's FANTABUMOUSE! I can use that recipe to make the **PERFECT CHOCOLATE CHEESECAKE**. Mice will come from miles away just to buy it. Mark my whiskers, I'll be RICH, RICH, RICH!"

I HAVE A
LITTLE PLAN

My **heart** sank.

Now what were we going to do? Squeaks would never give up the painting. And what about SWEET Perky Le Mouse?

I was anxiously chewing on my pawnail when Hercule smacked me.

"Listen up, Geronimo," he whispered. "**I have a little plan.**"

UH-OH.

The last time I helped Hercule with one of his little plans, I ended up out on a window ledge on the fifty-first floor of a high-rise apartment building! But that's another story.

Now Hercule leaned in close. "Okay, here's what we're going to do. I'll **trip** Squeaks.

You **trip** the butler. I'll grab Perky. You grab the painting. Then off we go," he said.

I looked doubtful.

"Trust me, Geronimo," Hercule insisted. "Have I ever messed things up before?"

I was about to remind him about the scary window-ledge incident when Hercule took off.

He barged into the room **shouting**, "Have no fear, Hercule Poirat is here!"

I ran after him.

What else could I do?

"Um, every rodent look this way — Geronimo here to save the day," I squeaked.

Pretty cheesy, I know. But I was never very good at rhyming. At least it got me noticed.

Sugarhog's butler reached for me, but I

quickly stuck out my paw. He tripped and went sprawling into the cheese soup. Hercule tripped Squeaks. The big mouse fell snout-first onto the hard tile floor. His eyes rolled  back in his head. But before he fainted he muttered, "Have a nice swim!"

Just then, I saw his paw reach for something under the table. He pushed a hidden BUTTON. A trapdoor opened. Hercule grabbed Perky. I grabbed the PAINTING. A minute later, we all tumbled down . . . down . . . down . . . into a giant vat of cream cheese!

Hmmm. All of this swimming around in cheese was really making me hungry!

SAFE!

In the end, Squeaks had actually helped make our *GETAWAY* easier. No one drowned in the vat of cream cheese. In fact, that cream cheese was pretty tasty. If I had a bagel and a cup of coffee, it would have been perfect. But there was no time to waste. We hurried out of the factory and called the police. They ARRESTED Squeaks and his butler and threw them both in jail. *The Celebration of Chocolate Cheesecake* and Perky Le Mouse were safe!

The following day, Perky cleaned off the cream cheese from the painting just in time for the big unveiling.

Kristina Colorsnout was thrilled. "How can I ever thank you two?" she asked.

I started to tell her she didn't need to thank us, but Hercule pushed me aside.

"Well, if you could just put in a **good word** with my Granny Ironwhiskers, I'd appreciate it," he mumbled.

Ms. Colorsnout chuckled. "No problem," she squeaked.

Twenty minutes later, I stood among the crowd in the banquet hall of the museum. What an exciting moment! The beautifully restored *Celebration of Chocolate Cheesecake* was about to be unveiled. Hercule strode up to the podium with the COVERED painting.

"I am happy to announce that Pierre Passionpaw's most treasured work of art has found its way home," he squeaked. Thunderous applause filled the room.

"I'd like to thank Ms. Colorsnout for letting

me work on such an EXCITING case," Hercule continued. "And I'd also like to thank my dear friend, Geronimo Stilton. Without Geronimo's encouragement, trust, and steadfast loyalty, I would have never solved this **M**y**st**e**r**y."

The crowd began to cheer and chant:

"Geronimo! Geronimo!"

I turned **beet-red** with embarrassment.

Did you know that I am a shy mouse at heart?

Hercule waved me up to the stage. Then together we unveiled the painting.

"**Ahhhhhhhhhhhh!**" the crowd gasped.

The Celebration of Chocolate Cheesecake really is a **breathtaking** picture.

Grant Gentlemouse and his bride, Glitterfur, look so in *love*. Oh, how amazing it must feel to find the mouse of your dreams. Of course, that got me thinking about Petunia Pretty Paws. She was such an amazing mouse. Too bad I had **messed** up our *Valentine's Day* date. I wondered if she'd ever forgive me.

I was still pining over Petunia when Kristina Colorsnout's *cheerful* voice snapped me back to the present.

MAY I ASK YOU A HUGE FAVOR?

"Mr. Stilton, I was wondering if you would do me a **HUGE** favor. I was told you're a remarkable *gourmet food* connoisseur," Kristina said.

I was shocked. I mean, don't get me wrong. I love fine food as much as the next mouse, but I also **love** the kind of mac and cheese that comes in a box. Don't tell my snobby Auntie Pearl Whiskers, though. She would be highly offended.

Anyway, Kristina must have sensed my **SURPRISE** because she put her paw on my shoulder.

"No need to be modest, Mr. Stilton. I was just chatting with a lovely mouse named

Petunia Pretty Paws. She told me you're a very **intelligent**, very *sophisticated*, very talented, and very distinguished rodent. A rodent who's an **EXPERT** on just about everything," she explained.

I grinned. As I said, I know next to **nothing** about gourmet cooking, but I was absolutely thrilled Petunia had said such nice things about me. Maybe she would forgive me after all. Maybe she would agree to go on another date with me. It could be a do-over *Valentine's Day* date. And this time, I would make sure I was on time. I would buy flowers or maybe an **enormous** box of chocolate cheesy chews.

"Well, I wouldn't say I'm an expert, though I do know my way around the kitchen a bit," I said. "Did Petunia really say all those nice things about me?"

"Of course she did! She told me you would be able to help me with my little problem." she persisted. "May I ask you a huge favor?"

"Of course," I agreed. I was so excited about a future date with Petunia I would have agreed to anything.

Kristina drew a deep sigh of relief. Then she **grabbed** me by the paw and dragged me onstage.

A horrified feeling crept over me. What was I doing up on the stage? What on earth had I just agreed to do? Why had I said yes?

At that moment, Kristina held up a paw.

"Everyone, please listen up!" she squealed, addressing the crowd.

Silence filled the room.

"We have a big surprise on tonight's program. Unfortunately, the judges for our annual cooking contest have all come down with a stomach bug and will be unable to make it," she began.

THE CROWD GROANED.

"But there is no need to worry!" she assured them. "Mr. Geronimo Stilton has agreed to take their place! Mr. Stilton is not only a very intelligent, sophisticated, talented, and distinguished rodent, but he is also an *expert* gourmet connoisseur!"

The crowd went wild.

"**Geronimo! Geronimo!**" they chanted again.

I felt **FAINT**.

It was then that I noticed a **long line of chefs** filing up to the stage for the **cooking contest**. Each one held a dish in his or her paws. I stretched my neck to see where the line of chefs ended, but it never did. It wrapped around and around the room, then went out the door. Yikes! How many dishes was I supposed to **taste**?

Kristina led me over to a long table already filled with food. "Tonight, the top one hundred **cooks** on Mouse Island will compete for the title of BEST COOK OF THE YEAR. And since we are also here to honor the historic masterpiece *The Celebration of Chocolate Cheesecake*, I though it was only fitting that we do just that — CELEBRATE CHEESECAKE. Yes, my dear friends, Geronimo Stilton will now taste one hundred samples of **CHOCOLATE**

CHEESECAKE!" she announced.

My jaw hit the ground. No, I wasn't getting ready to inhale my first piece of cheesecake, I was in shock. One hundred pieces of cheesecake? Had everyone gone mad? No mouse could eat that much! Suddenly, I felt sick just thinking about eating. Plus, did I mention I have a weak stomach?

"Here you go, Mr. Stilton," Kristina squeaked. "Please sit here and start tasting." She ushered me into a chair. Then she handed me an enormouse PILL. "This will help you DIGEST when you're finished," she whispered. "Trust me, you're going to need it."

I felt like screaming. I felt like crying. I felt like jumping off that stage and hopping the next plane to Sunnysqueak Island. Oh, what I wouldn't give to be lying on a warm sandy beach without a cheesecake in sight!

"Sound the trumpets!" Kristina Colorsnout shouted. "DRUMROLL, please!"

I opened my mouth to protest. "Actually, I know very little about cooking," I admitted. "Oh, come now," she replied. "There's no need to be modest, Mr. Stilton!"

Before I knew it, Kristina stuck a forkful of cheesecake in my mouth.

THen anotHer.

AnD anotHer!

HAPPY BIRTHDAY, GERONIMO!

When I got home, I **collapsed** into my bed. It was only 8:30, but I was dead tired.

Just then, the doorbell rang.

What now? I moaned. Couldn't a mouse get some peace?

I **DRAGGED** myself to the door, half asleep.

When I opened it, I could hardly believe my eyes. There were all my friends and relatives: Trap, Thea, Benjamin, Petunia, Bugsy Wugsy, Grandfather William, Aunt Sweetfur, Hercule Poirat, and more.

They all **shouted** together,

"Happy Birthday, Geronimo!"

I slapped a paw to my forehead. Holey cheese! I had been so busy eating cheesecake, I had forgotten today was my birthday!

The crowd spilled into my living room.

I wanted to crawl under the couch. I was still dressed in my pajamas and slippers!

"We brought you a very special birthday cake, Gerrykins," my cousin Trap chuckled. Then he wheeled a GIANT cake into the room.

I gulped. Do you know what kind of cake it was? You guessed it. **CHOCOLATE CHEESECAKE**.

First I blew out the candles. Then everyone started chanting, "Take a bite! Take a bite!"

I stared at the cheesecake, feeling ill. But, just at that moment, I noticed Petunia Pretty

Paws. "Happy Birthday, Geronimo," she whispered. At that moment, Hercule emerged from the crowd. "I told Petunia it was my fault you missed your Valentine's Day date with her," Hercule explained. Petunia **smiled** at me shyly.

Suddenly, I felt like I could do **ANYTHING**. I grabbed my fork and took a big bite of cheesecake. And you know what?

It tasted great!

I smiled back at Petunia, and together we cut the rest of the cheesecake.

I was glad Petunia had forgiven **me** for our disastrous Valentine's Day date. She really is an amazing mouse. Who knows? Maybe I'll get the chance to take her out on another date soon. After all, **Saint Patrick's Day** is coming up. And then there's Be Kind to Your Fur Day. I know, I know, those **holidays** aren't half as special as *Valentine's Day*. But a mouse has to start somewhere!

Tips for
Organizing an
Exciting

Cheesecake Party!

Chocolate Cheesecake

INGREDIENTS:

CRUST:
1½ cups chocolate wafer crumbs • ¼ teaspoon ground cinnamon • 6 tablespoons butter or margarine, melted

FILLING:
4 8-ounce packages cream cheese, softened • 1 cup sugar • 1 tablespoon flour • 5 eggs • ½ cup sour cream • 12 ounces semisweet chocolate chips, melted • 2 teaspoons vanilla extract

TO PREPARE CRUST:

1. Mix the chocolate wafer crumbs and cinnamon.
2. Add melted butter or margarine to crumb mixture and mix with a fork until completely moistened.
3. Press mixture into the bottom and up ⅓ of the sides of a 9-inch springform pan.
4. Bake crust at 350°F for 10 minutes.

TO PREPARE FILLING:

1. Mix together cream cheese and sugar until well blended.

2. Beat in flour.

3. Add eggs one at a time, mixing well.

4. Beat in sour cream.

5. Blend in the melted chocolate and vanilla.

6. Pour into prepared crust.

7. Bake at 425°F for 15 minutes, then lower oven to 300°F. Bake for an additional 45 minutes.

8. Turn off the oven and allow the cake to cool in the oven for an hour.

9. Remove from oven and cool completely. Refrigerate overnight. (Serves 12)

Before cooking,
always ask an
adult for help.

Berry Cheesecake Pie

INGREDIENTS:

- 1 8-ounce package cream cheese, softened
- ¾ cup sifted confectioners' sugar, plus additional for sprinkling
- 1 teaspoon vanilla extract
- 1 cup whipped cream
- 1 9-inch pre-made graham cracker pie shell
- 1 pint strawberries, washed and cut in half

1. Beat together cream cheese, sugar, and vanilla until smooth.

2. Fold in whipped cream.

3. Spoon into prepared pie shell.

4. Chill until set. Just before serving, top pie with halved berries, placing them cut-side down.

5. Sprinkle with additional confectioners' sugar, if you wish.

Mock Candy Decorations

- Crepe paper in different colors
- Newspaper
- Colored ribbons
- Round pointed scissors
- Stapler & string

1. Cut several 4-inch by 8-inch rectangles of crepe paper.

2. Take the newspaper sheets and cut them into small pieces, which you will crush into small balls.

3. Fill the crepe rectangles with the newspaper balls.

4. Tie each decoration at both ends with the colored ribbon as if it is a hard candy.

5. Once all the rectangles have been cut and filled, staple the "candies" to a string to make a festive decoration.

Let's Play Together!

WHAT YOU NEED:

As many pens and sheets of paper as there are players.

A stopwatch or a timer.

RULES OF THE GAME:

(1) Each player should draw six columns on his or her sheet.

(2) An adult can be a timekeeper, or select someone from the group.

(3) Label each column with a category the group chooses to compete in. For example: animals, cities, desserts, actors/actresses, sports, films, books, fruit, etc.

(4) Pick a letter of the alphabet. Each player tries to write as many words beginning with that letter in three minutes.

(5) After the round is complete, choose another letter of the alphabet and play the next round!

SCORING:

Whoever gives an original answer in that category (an answer given by no one else), earns 10 points. If someone else had the same answer, each person gets 5 points. Whoever accumulates the most points after six rounds wins.

Want to read my next adventure?
It's sure to be a fur-raising experience!

THE RACE ACROSS AMERICA

I, Geronimo Stilton, am not a big fan of races. I like to take my time and smell the cheese! But when my friend Bruce Pawstrong invited me to race across America on my bicycle, I just couldn't resist. And holey cheese, what a fabumouse adventure we had!

And don't miss any of my other fabumouse adventures!

#1 LOST TREASURE OF THE EMERALD EYE

#2 THE CURSE OF THE CHEESE PYRAMID

#3 CAT AND MOUSE IN A HAUNTED HOUSE

#4 I'M TOO FOND OF MY FUR!

#5 FOUR MICE DEEP IN THE JUNGLE

#6 PAWS OFF, CHEDDARFACE!

#7 RED PIZZAS FOR A BLUE COUNT

#8 ATTACK OF THE BANDIT CATS

#9 A FABUMOUSE VACATION FOR GERONIMO

#10 ALL BECAUSE OF A CUP OF COFFEE

#11 IT'S HALLOWEEN, YOU 'FRAIDY MOUSE!

#12 MERRY CHRISTMAS, GERONIMO!

#13 THE PHANTOM OF THE SUBWAY

#14 THE TEMPLE OF THE RUBY OF FIRE

#15 THE MONA MOUSA CODE

#16 A CHEESE-COLORED CAMPER

#17 WATCH YOUR WHISKERS, STILTON!

#18 SHIPWRECK ON THE PIRATE ISLANDS

#19 MY NAME IS STILTON, GERONIMO STILTON

#20 SURF'S UP, GERONIMO!

#21 THE WILD, WILD WEST

#22 THE SECRET OF CACKLEFUR CASTLE

A CHRISTMAS TALE

#23 VALENTINE'S DAY DISASTER

#24 FIELD TRIP TO NIAGARA FALLS

#25 THE SEARCH FOR SUNKEN TREASURE

#26 THE MUMMY WITH NO NAME

#27 THE CHRISTMAS TOY FACTORY

#28 WEDDING CRASHER

#29 DOWN AND OUT DOWN UNDER

#30 THE MOUSE ISLAND MARATHON

#31 THE MYSTERIOUS CHEESE THIEF

CHRISTMAS CATASTROPHE

#32 VALLEY OF THE GIANT SKELETONS

#33 GERONIMO AND THE GOLD MEDAL MYSTERY

#34 GERONIMO STILTON, SECRET AGENT

#35 A VERY MERRY CHRISTMAS

And don't forget to look for

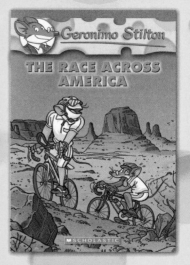

#37 THE RACE ACROSS AMERICA

ABOUT THE AUTHOR

Born in New Mouse City, Mouse Island, Geronimo Stilton is Rattus Emeritus of Mousomorphic Literature and of Neo-Ratonic Comparative Philosophy. For the past twenty years, he has been running *The Rodent's Gazette,* New Mouse City's most widely read daily newspaper.

Stilton was awarded the Ratitzer Prize for his scoops on *The Curse of the Cheese Pyramid* and *The Search for Sunken Treasure.* He has also received the Andersen 2000 Prize for Personality of the Year. One of his bestsellers won the 2002 eBook Award for world's best ratlings' electronic book. His works have been published all over the globe.

In his spare time, Mr. Stilton collects antique cheese rinds and plays golf. But what he most enjoys is telling stories to his nephew Benjamin.

THE RODENT'S GAZETTE

1. Main entrance
2. Printing presses (where the books and newspaper are printed)
3. Accounts department
4. Editorial room (where the editors, illustrators, and designers work)
5. Geronimo Stilton's office
6. Storage space for Geronimo's books

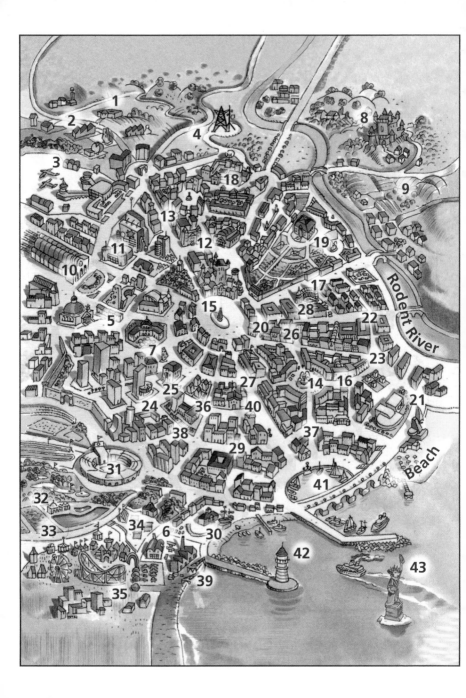

Map of New Mouse City

1. Industrial Zone
2. Cheese Factories
3. Angorat International Airport
4. WRAT Radio and Television Station
5. Cheese Market
6. Fish Market
7. Town Hall
8. Snotnose Castle
9. The Seven Hills of Mouse Island
10. Mouse Central Station
11. Trade Center
12. Movie Theater
13. Gym
14. Catnegie Hall
15. Singing Stone Plaza
16. The Gouda Theater
17. Grand Hotel
18. Mouse General Hospital
19. Botanical Gardens
20. Cheap Junk for Less (Trap's store)
21. Parking Lot
22. Mouseum of Modern Art
23. University and Library
24. *The Daily Rat*
25. *The Rodent's Gazette*
26. Trap's House
27. Fashion District
28. The Mouse House Restaurant
29. Environmental Protection Center
30. Harbor Office
31. Mousidon Square Garden
32. Golf Course
33. Swimming Pool
34. Blushing Meadow Tennis Courts
35. Curlyfur Island Amusement Park
36. Geronimo's House
37. New Mouse City Historic District
38. Public Library
39. Shipyard
40. Thea's House
41. New Mouse Harbor
42. Luna Lighthouse
43. The Statue of Liberty

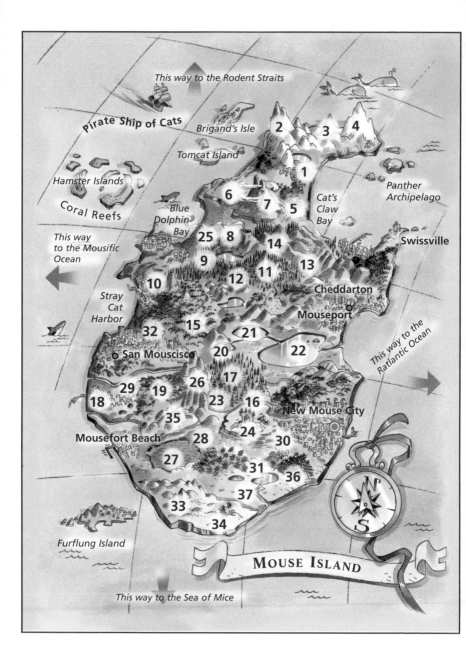

Map of Mouse Island

1. Big Ice Lake
2. Frozen Fur Peak
3. Slipperyslopes Glacier
4. Coldcreeps Peak
5. Ratzikistan
6. Transratania
7. Mount Vamp
8. Roastedrat Volcano
9. Brimstone Lake
10. Poopedcat Pass
11. Stinko Peak
12. Dark Forest
13. Vain Vampires Valley
14. Goose Bumps Gorge
15. The Shadow Line Pass
16. Penny Pincher Castle
17. Nature Reserve Park
18. Las Ratayas Marinas
19. Fossil Forest
20. Lake Lake
21. Lake Lakelake
22. Lake Lakelakelake
23. Cheddar Crag
24. Cannycat Castle
25. Valley of the Giant Sequoia
26. Cheddar Springs
27. Sulfurous Swamp
28. Old Reliable Geyser
29. Vole Vale
30. Ravingrat Ravine
31. Gnat Marshes
32. Munster Highlands
33. Mousehara Desert
34. Oasis of the Sweaty Camel
35. Cabbagehead Hill
36. Rattytrap Jungle
37. Rio Mosquito

Dear mouse friends,
Thanks for reading, and farewell
till the next book.
It'll be another whisker-licking-good
adventure, and that's a promise!

Geronimo Stilton